TARGET

THE ALTERNATIVE

TARGET

PATRICK JONES

darbycreek
MINNEAPOLIS

Darby Creek
A division of Lerner Publishing Group, Inc.
241 First Avenue North
Minneapolis, MN 55401 U.S.A.

For updated reading levels and more information, look up this title at www.lernerbooks.com.

Cover and interior photographs © Mona Makela/Dreamstime.com (boy); © iStockphoto.com/joeygil (locker background).

Main body text set in Janson Text LT Std 12/17.
Typeface provided by Linotype AG.

Library of Congress Cataloging-in-Publication Data

Jones, Patrick, 1961–
Target / by Patrick Jones.
pages cm. — (The alternative)
Summary: When seventeen-year-old Frankie Smith's incarcerated father and cousins try to get him involved in the First Nation Mafia, even after his mother enrolls Frankie in an alternative high school to keep him safe, Frankie has a hard choice to make.
ISBN 978-1-4677-3900-9 (lib. bdg. : alk. paper)
ISBN 978-1-4677-4633-5 (eBook)
[1. Gangs—Fiction. 2. Conduct of life—Fiction. 3. High schools—Fiction. 4. Schools—Fiction. 5. Native Americans—Minnesota—Fiction. 6. Family problems—Fiction.] I. Title.
PZ7.J7242Tar 2014
[Fic]—dc23 2013041393

Manufactured in the United States of America
1 – BP – 7/15/14

WITH THANKS TO BRIANNA, KIARA, NAYALIE,
AND VINCENTE

—P. J.

1

Frankie Smith took his time unpacking his few belongings into the tiny bedroom of the apartment on St. Paul's east side. After years of moving in and out of double-wide trailers and rented houses on the Riverwood Reservation, he wondered if living in a crowded high-rise in a big city would be weird. Frankie's mom said they were in St. Paul to be close to his father, but Frankie knew it was also to get him away from his friends.

"How's it going?" Frankie's mother yelled from the other room. Frankie didn't answer.

He'd given her the silent treatment the whole three-hour drive from the reservation; it was one of his few weapons. She already knew people, had a job, and had a plan for them: "We're starting over, Frankie, starting over."

Frankie wasn't interested in starting over. He was even less interested in starting next week at a big urban high school. There was nothing school could teach him more than the streets or his grandfather, a Dakota tribal elder.

His mom knocked gently on the door, but Frankie didn't open it. He wouldn't let her in: his door, his business, his life. "Frankie, hurry up and get dressed, or we'll be late to see your father."

Frankie sat on the bed and looked east out of the eighth-story window. He'd never lived this high up before. Moving slowly, he unpacked his three prized possessions. The first was a handwritten, framed prayer from Chief Yellow Lark that his grandfather had made for him. The second was the best book he'd ever read, which also happened to be the only one he'd ever finished: *The Outsiders*, by S. E. Hinton.

The action-packed story of "greasers" and "socs" appealed to Frankie, even though the book didn't seem that realistic. These weren't real gangs like he knew in Riverwood. Gangs settled scores not with fists, but guns. Guns like his third possession: his dad's pearl-handled revolver.

2

"Frankie!" some guy shouted over booming bass outside Frankie's building. Frankie turned to look as he reached the front door, carrying one of their last boxes from the move.

Frankie's instincts told him to run, but before he could move, the car came to a stop. "Frankie, I heard you were coming to town." The passenger door opened, and a tall kid with short black hair, acne, and dark sunglasses emerged. "It's me. Billy."

Frankie took a step toward the car—a beat-up Buick that looked older than he was—as the driver's door opened. Same basic look, but longer hair and better skin. "Forget your cousins already, Frankie?" the driver said.

With a quick nod and smile, Frankie stretched out his hands, but the twins took turns wrapping him in a bear hug. They smelled of cigarettes. "Jay! Good to see you guys."

Even as the words left his mouth, he wasn't really sure. His mom wanted him to start over here, but that would be difficult if he got involved with members of his dad's side of the family.

"Get in, let us show you the hood," Jay said. "It's ours for the taking."

Frankie reluctantly climbed into the backseat of the clunker. His mouth felt dry from the smoke inhabiting every crevice of the torn upholstery. "For the taking?"

"They locked up all the OGs, cuz. There's a need for new blood," Jay continued. "The new chiefs are going to need all the braves they can get. You're in, right?"

Jay rolled up his sleeve to show Frankie his First Nation Mafia tattoo. Frankie had seen plenty of them before at his old school, at home, and briefly on his own left arm, before his mom forced him to have it removed. The area still stung, especially when he was sweating—like in the beat-up car, keeping his arm covered. He also kept his mouth shut as Jay explained that the recent imprisonment of thirty older leaders of the First Nation Mafia meant there was a power vacuum. “But you gotta prove yourself, cuz,” Jay said. “Don’t matter what you did at Riverwood. It’s like starting over.”

3

"Really, Frankie, the first day?" Frankie's mom sighed as she sat with him outside the Harding High assistant principal's office. With her piercing brown eyes, long black hair, and radiant smile, Frankie's mom oozed both sweetness and confidence to outsiders. But she didn't hide her bitterness about how fast Frankie had found trouble.

"What is it *this* time?" Unlike his dad, who would've slapped him with an open palm, Frankie's mom used her words, her tone, and her manner as discipline.

"Some snot-nosed kid was trying to prove himself on the first day." What Frankie said was partially true—except he was the one trying to prove himself, and Jay and Billy had picked out his target. "I'll only miss school for a few days."

"I bet the other kid will miss his front teeth for longer," his mom snapped. Another deep sigh. Then, "Frankie, you promised, remember?"

Frankie nodded. Before he'd stopped all but essential communication, he had promised his mom he'd stop getting in trouble.

"It's not the promise you made to *me*," his mom said. "But to my father. You dishonor not just yourself, but your grandfather. If you dishonor him, you dishonor all our ancestors."

Frankie stared at the wall to avoid his mom's eyes.

"Were Jay and Billy there?" his mom asked.

Frankie shrugged.

"I warned you not to hang around with them, didn't I?"

"Mom, you tell me so much stuff to do and not do that I can't keep it all straight."

Frankie's mom rolled her eyes and tugged

at her ID badge for work. "Simple. Stay out of trouble. Period."

Just then the assistant principal, an older white guy with a beer belly and crew cut, waddled through his doorway. "Are you Frankie's mother?" the AP asked. Frankie's mom nodded and sighed again, like it hurt to admit it.

4

Corn chips, Pepsi, and the TV remote had kept Frankie busy most of the week. He'd served out his four-day suspension from Harding, although he wasn't going back. His mom had decided to move him to Rondo Alternative High School to avoid Billy and Jay. She'd also called their mother and told her to keep them away from her son.

"You there, cuz?" Frankie heard Jay shout from the hallway. Frankie tossed the remote on the sofa and headed for the apartment door. Peeking out, Frankie saw his cousins waiting.

He paused before he opened the door to them. After an exchange of fist bumps, Billy and Jay made their way into the room.

"Guys, you're not supposed to be here," Frankie said. "My mom said that—"

The twins laughed, and Jay cut him off. "Aww, his mom said . . . What are you, five?"

"I'm just surprised to see you. I thought she talked to your mom about it," Frankie said as his cousins sat on the sofa.

"Mom doesn't remember much." Billy mimicked someone drinking. "Not much at all."

Frankie moved to the kitchen table and picked up one of his mother's business cards from her new job. He handed it to Billy. Billy looked it over, laughed, and handed it to his brother.

"Thanks, but our mom's been to plenty of—" Jay stopped and examined the business card. "Plenty of chemical dependency counselors. It don't stick."

"Hey, good thing you ain't coming back to Harding," Billy said. "Seems that guy we had you pop was some big deal in the Twenty-sixers."

"Twenty-sixers?" Frankie repeated.

"The Latino gang pinching in on us," Jay said. "I smoothed it out, but if I was you, I'd be careful." Frankie nodded.

"Seen your dad? How is he?" Billy asked.

Frankie moved to the door and opened it, annoyed with the question. He glanced in the mirror by the door and saw his father's cold stare looking back at him. "Same as always," Frankie answered.

5

Rondo Alternative High School didn't look like any school Frankie had ever seen. The school shared a building with a hockey rink, and the small classrooms and smaller conference rooms made him feel like a giant. At Riverwood there was so much space, but in St. Paul it seemed everything was jammed together. Especially when he was stuck in an office with four adults.

"Good afternoon, Frankie," said Mrs. Baker, the principal. Another man and woman smiled, nodded, and also welcomed Frankie and his mother. New in her job, Frankie's mom couldn't take time off work, so they were meeting to enroll him over her lunch hour.

Frankie's mom, as always, had lots of questions, and Frankie pretended to pay attention while he sized up the principal and teachers: Mrs. Baker, young and hot; Mr. Aaron, a school aide who was kinda old but seemed cool; and Mrs. Howard-Hernandez, not as young, talked too much about reading.

"Frankie, is there anything you want to add?" Mrs. Baker asked.

"You got Internet?" Frankie replied, recovering from his daze. "We don't have none at the crib."

Mrs. Baker nodded. "We make broad use of online resources in our learning environment," she said.

Frankie raised an eyebrow. "You could've just said yes."

Mr. Aaron laughed. *That guy might be okay*, Frankie thought.

"We've yet to receive your transcripts from Riverwood High School, so tell us a little bit about yourself," Mrs. Baker said. "Favorite subjects, favorite books?"

Frankie felt uncomfortable in the hard green chair. "I don't like to read."

Mrs. Howard-Hernandez chimed in. "I'm the language arts teacher, so I take that as a challenge," she said, smiling.

"Frankie, don't be shy," his mom said, but Frankie wished he were anywhere but in that chair.

"Really, there's nothing you'd like to share with us?" Mrs. Baker asked.

Frankie met her pleasant expression with a tensed jaw. "Only subject I care about is history—my family's history."

6

"Who's the hottie?" Frankie asked the kid sitting next to him in fifth-period language arts, motioning to the girl a few seats ahead. Frankie didn't take his eyes off her curves. "She got a boyfriend?"

"Dude, that's my cousin Sofia, so watch it," the guy said, but he laughed when he said it.

"Man, sorry, my bad," Frankie said, laughing as well, finally breaking his stare. "Frankie Smith." He offered his fist.

"Luis Martinez," the guy said and accepted the fist bump. "No worries."

"What you in for?" Frankie whispered, since Mrs. Howard-Hernandez had started talking.

Luis laughed again. "It's a school, not a prison. Though sometimes it's hard to tell the difference." Frankie didn't say anything. Luis obviously hadn't been to a real prison.

"We have a new student today," the teacher said. "Frankie, anything you'd like to say?"

"I used to live up in Riverwood." The teacher waited for more, but Frankie just stared at her. His history was nobody's business.

"Frankie told me he's not much of a reader, but we'll see about that," said Mrs. Howard-Hernandez, smiling. "So, what is the last book you read?"

In his head, Frankie had already renamed her Mrs. Shut Your Face Please. "*The Outsiders*," he mumbled. He expected some giggles, but no one laughed. The teacher walked to an over-stuffed bookcase, examined a shelf, and pulled out a worn paperback copy of the book.

"'When I stepped out into the bright sun-light, from the darkness of the movie house, I had only two things on my mind: Paul Newman, and a ride home,'" the teacher read aloud.

"I got a question," Luis spoke up. "Who the hell is Paul Newman?" Everybody laughed.

"Frankie?" the teacher asked. Frankie shrugged as the laughter became directed at him.

"There's your first assignment, Frankie," the teacher said. "For next week: Who is Paul Newman?"

7

"Frankie, get in quick," Billy shouted from the passenger side of a newish SUV.

Frankie was out on the sidewalk in front of their apartment building late on Friday evening, just to get away from his mom. Their apartment seemed so small when she was home. He wanted to get fresh air in his lungs, although the streets of east St. Paul seemed always to be filled with truck exhaust fumes. "Get in!" Jay yelled. "Move!"

Frankie had gotten through his first week at Rondo without getting in trouble, so he thought he'd earned a reward of some sort. He was ready for whatever excitement the twins had in store.

"Where'd you get the ride?" Frankie asked. Jay just giggled, which told Frankie all he needed to know about the answer.

With the music loud, Jay drove Frankie through the neighborhood, pointing out which corners belonged to the First Nation Mafia and which ones the 26ers held. Frankie grunted every now and then, pretending to be interested, but he wasn't. Maybe his mom was right. He could start over: new city, new school, new friends. Maybe a new girlfriend.

"So like we said, you gotta start small and prove yourself," Billy said. "You give us thirty percent of what you sell, but then we kick part of that up to the new chiefs. That's how it works."

Frankie said nothing, but he felt his empty pockets and heard his growling stomach and knew he didn't have much of a choice.

Billy turned and handed Frankie a pair of sunglasses and two large sacks. "You best put your seatbelt on, cuz," Billy said. "Or you'll fly through the windshield like an arrow."

Frankie buckled up and started to speak, but he was interrupted by the jarring force, the crashing of metal, and the shattering of glass as the SUV plowed into a closed corner store. When the SUV came to rest, Billy and Jay leaped from the vehicle. Frankie followed, dazed and scared.

"Grab as much as you can, mostly cigarettes, that's where the money is!" Jay yelled.

In a single minute, Frankie and the twins filled up sacks with cigarettes as the security alarm blared. Then the three raced toward the beat-up Buick parked down the block.

8

"Remember, there are rules we'll need to follow," Frankie's mom said as they exited the interstate.

Frankie laughed to himself: his mom never met a rule she didn't follow, and his dad never met one he didn't try to break. As his mom reminded him of the visiting rules, Frankie pretended to listen, but mostly he nodded in time to the music playing from the new iPod in his pocket and bud in his right ear. Even after kicking back thirty percent, selling smokes at Rondo was profitable, both in dollars and in friends. *Too bad Sofia doesn't smoke*, Frankie thought. He'd need to find another way to get close to her.

"Frankie, are you listening?" He heard his mom ask.

"Yeah." Frankie smiled, nodded, and turned down the volume.

"I'm glad this new school is working out. Do you like it?"

"I guess." Frankie didn't want to admit he liked Rondo—anything he liked was something his mom could take away if he got busted or if she found the iPod and asked questions.

"Are you making some friends?"

Frankie tried not to laugh. "Quite a few." He figured loyal customers counted.

"I'm glad you aren't hanging around Jay and Billy anymore. They're a bad influence. It's not all their fault—their mother . . ."

Frankie turned the music up. He didn't want to hear about parental influence, especially on the way to see his dad. They were going to visit him four times every week: Saturday and Sunday afternoons and Thursday and Friday nights. The regular visiting hours at Stillwater State Prison.

9

Half an hour later, Frankie hid the iPod under the car seat and then handed his mom everything else.

"Let's go, Frankie, the line here is terrible on Sundays," his mother said. Frankie nodded and fell in behind. The security check at Stillwater was the harshest he'd gone through in years of visiting his dad at various jails, county correctional facilities, and halfway houses. Frankie's dad, Franklin Brave Eagle Smith, had spent more time behind bars than free during his son's life. But his recent conviction, as one of the First Nation Mafia chiefs, meant he would be in prison until he either died of old age or was targeted by a rival gang.

"I hate this," Frankie mumbled as they entered the crowded waiting area. They joined a long, winding line for the security check. While Frankie's mom placed her keys and purse in the locker, Frankie examined the sea of faces around them: young, old, and oldest, all different colors. There were crying babies, bored teens, and one babbling older man. But mostly it was women, ladies like his mother, who stood by her man, no matter what.

"I'm sorry, Frankie, did you say something?" his mom asked when she returned.

"I said I hate this."

Frankie's mom nodded, and an out-of-place smile spread across her face.

"What are you smiling about?" Frankie asked. When they visited his dad, his mom rarely smiled or even spoke, acting like it almost hurt.

She didn't answer—just eyed Frankie, still smiling.

"Come on, why are you smiling?"

"You said you hated this, right?" Frankie's mom asked.

Frankie nodded. Like everything else in St. Paul, the lobby was crowded and noisy.

Frankie's mom leaned in toward him and put her hands on his shoulders. Then she lightly brushed his long black hair out of his face. "Good. It's jail. You're supposed to hate it."

10

Frankie cradled the tan visitation phone in his hand. Everything in the Stillwater State Prison visiting area was the same: tan, dirty, and gritty. Phone in hand, Frankie wondered how many other sons had used it to speak to their dads, or the other way around. In the Smith line, the male roots of the family tree were firmly planted in corrections. Except nothing ever got corrected. Year after year, generation after generation, the Smith men ended up behind bars.

"How is school?" Frankie's father asked in his familiar raspy voice.

His father's interest in his schooling was surprising and new. "Okay, I guess."

"You connected with Jay and Billy Creech?" Frankie's father asked. "You need your brothers to protect you out there, like I do in here." Frankie hesitated before answering.

Even through the glass, Franklin Smith's eyes burned dark. To Frankie, it seemed his father's eyes had turned from brown to black over the years, especially when he stared hard at his son.

"Listen, bad things are going down," Frankie's dad said. "You keep the twins close, you hear?"

Frankie nodded, breaking his father's stare. But it wasn't just the stare. Everything about his dad—including a three-inch scar visible on his newly shaved head—told the world that Franklin Brave Eagle Smith was a man to be feared, respected, and avoided.

"Why did you shave your head?" Frankie asked.

"I took my hair before the white men here could," his father answered. "Like they took everything else from us." He looked down and then looked straight at Frankie. "Even when we rose up, formed a new tribe, then the white men called us gangsters and locked us up."

Frankie avoided his dad's stare. His grandfather saw it differently—thought his dad wasn't a leader of a new tribe, he was a criminal. Who was Franklin Brave Eagle Smith, really? If he had to keep spending weekends in Stillwater, Frankie hoped these visits would help him decide for himself.

11

The visit with his dad lasted the whole hour that was allowed. Then visits with Jay and Billy's father, and four other family members, lasted another three. Half a Sunday spent in Stillwater seemed like forever. "I need to stop at a library," Frankie told his mom as they left the prison parking lot.

The request earned a double take from his mom, but she agreed, and Frankie mumbled, "Thanks." He clicked on the music as they drove out of the prison's shadow into a bright fall afternoon.

The fast-food lunch they'd gotten on the way to Stillwater didn't sit well in Frankie's stomach. Nor did the ongoing conversation with his mother—although *conversation* was the wrong word, since Frankie rarely spoke. He listened, nodded, and repeated back as needed from his mom's endless lecture on how Frankie would be different, how he wouldn't repeat his father's and uncles' mistakes. He would stay free.

Inside the library, Frankie and his mom asked to get a library card.

"Your name, please?" asked the librarian.

Frankie started to speak but then stopped.

"Frankie, tell the woman—" his mom said.

Frankie handed the white woman behind the desk his Rondo ID. "Frankie Brave Eagle."

The woman looked at the ID. "That's not what it says here," she said, confused.

"Smith is the name white people gave my family. Brave Eagle is my real name," Frankie said.

His mother's irritation filled the small space. "Fine, use Brave Eagle." The woman typed the information into the computer and then handed

Frankie the card, which he signed Frankie Brave Eagle. He imagined his father's proud smile, somewhere in Stillwater.

"I'll be back in an hour. Is that enough time?" his mother asked.

Frankie nodded, and his mother took off. Frankie went to a computer station and printed off a web page on Paul Newman for his report. Then he returned to the desk.

"Can I help you?" the librarian asked

Frankie smiled. "Can I borrow some scissors?"

12

When his mom returned to the library and saw the hatchet job Frankie had done with the scissors, she refused to take him to a real barber. "Actions have consequences, Frankie, and now you look like a fool," she'd said. Instead, Frankie snuck out late that night, and his cousins shaved his head to finish the job.

At school, he waited until the end of the day to speak to Sofia so if she blew him off, he wouldn't reek of humiliation for six hours. "What do you think of my new look?" Frankie asked her.

Sofia clutched her books—way too many books—to her chest.

Frankie rubbed his fingers over his newly shaved head. "You wanna touch it? It's smooth."

"Like you?" she asked. The faintest smile broke on Sofia's face.

"Me? Smooth, no," Frankie's voice trembled.

"Well, you've made a lot of friends around here, Frankie Smith."

Frankie inched a little closer; she didn't back away. "What can I say? People like me."

Sofia laughed. "From what I hear, people mostly like your cheap cigarettes."

How can women slap a man so hard without raising a hand? Frankie wondered.

"You don't approve of smoking?" Frankie asked. "I just sell 'em, I don't use 'em."

Another laugh, smaller. "No, I don't approve of what you're doing. I'm not dumb."

Frankie moved another inch, closer. "I'm not either. I know you're about the smartest and prettiest girl here."

"Please, Frankie," Sofia said, books clutched tighter. "I know it's a gang thing." Frankie said nothing. Sofia pointed at the 26ers tattoo on her right arm. "I'm out, and I don't want anything to do with that life or anyone in it."

"But I'm not—" Frankie started, but Sofia turned on her high heels and walked away.

13

Frankie picked at his dinner of black beans and rice. While his mom had a good job counseling chemically dependent women, it didn't pay much. Rice and beans made up a good part of most meals.

"Aren't you hungry?" his mom asked.

"I'm not feeling well," Frankie mumbled. "I don't think I can go to school tomorrow."

"Your book report is due tomorrow. You'll be there." His mom's tone shifted, now harder.

"Maybe." Frankie shoveled food into his mouth to cover his I-got-caught grin.

"Frankie, I'm so pleased with the reports I'm getting from your teachers," his mom said with a new tone, one of pride. Frankie didn't hear it much, so he soaked it up. "You seem more focused. Why?"

"I don't know."

His mom sighed a classic mom sigh. "Come on." She waited. "No idea?"

Frankie scratched his head—it itched like crazy. His mom tapped her fork on his plate over and over, waiting for a response. "I don't know, Mom. The teachers at Rondo, they're different than my old teachers. Not better, just different. It's like they care more. About me."

His mom smiled like she'd won a big victory. "So you be different from the old Frankie—and go to school."

Frankie nodded. Truancy had been Frankie's best subject at Riverwood. The temptation of Sofia had made him want to go to class at Rondo until she'd rejected him.

"What do I get if I get an A?"

His mom smiled. "A proud mom. Now go finish your homework."

14

Frankie hardly looked up from his page—he didn't like speaking in front of the class and hadn't memorized the report. When he did glance up, he tried to make eye contact with Sofia. But she wasn't having it here, now, or any time or place. When Frankie tried to talk to her, she wouldn't say a word.

"So, that's my report," he finished.

A few kids clapped, including Luis and his friend Jose. Frankie started to retreat to his chair, but he got two steps away before Mrs. Howard-Hernandez stopped him with a question. "Frankie, what was the most interesting thing you learned about Paul Newman?"

Frankie looked down at the website printout. "A lot of stuff."

"Put the paper down," the teacher said. Frankie dumped the paper on his desk and slid into the chair. "Tell us what you think. Don't just tell us what you read about Paul Newman; tell us what you learned that you found interesting about him, that you'll use. Who you admire reveals a great deal about who you are and what you believe."

"Well, it was cool how he wasn't just an actor," Frankie said softly. "And then he was, like, freakin' rich and could have been richer, but he gave a lot of money he made to charity."

Mrs. Howard-Hernandez nodded. She seemed pleased.

"And what did you like least about him?"

"Well, in a movie called *Hombre*, he played an Indian. That's messed up." Frankie told the story of the movie, which he had read about on Wikipedia. "He was this Indian-raised white guy who, uh, faced prejudice when he returned to the white world for his inheritance after his dad died."

"Maybe we can show it in class," Mr. Aaron interjected from where he was sitting in with the class. "It's got a lot of action, which I know you all like, but the theme is pretty good too. It's about how people can change."

Frankie didn't know which caused him to smile more: what Mr. Aaron said or the B+ that Mrs. Howard-Hernandez wrote at the top of his paper. It was the best grade he'd ever received in English.

15

Frankie tried to keep calm as his father came into view, but his mother screamed. Two prison guards ran to her side and spoke with her while Frankie picked up the visitation phone.

"What happened to your eye?" Frankie asked, his voice trembling.

"A Twenty-sixer took it in a fight." Over his father's right eye was an eye patch. It wasn't black like a pirate patch—that would have been much better. It was a weird pinkish flesh color that looked like an empty socket.

"Did they get the guy?" *They*. The other

members of the First Nation Mafia.

His dad said nothing.

"Can you still see okay?" Frankie asked.

An unfamiliar smile came over Frankie's father's face. Years of fights, drugs, and alcohol abuse had destroyed his dad's mouth and face, along with the rest of his body. The missing eye was just the latest wound.

"You know of any of them?" his dad whispered into the phone. "Any Twenty-sixers?"

Frankie's blood turned icy.

"Frankie?" his dad repeated, still soft but commanding.

More silence from Frankie. He didn't want to hear any more. He turned to his mom, who was waiting off to the side. As he started to pull the phone away from his ear, he heard his dad say, "You know what to do, son. An eye for an eye."

Frankie dropped the phone. It bounced with a thud from the table. The sound echoed in the small space over the clamor of voices, along with the smack of Frankie's hard shoes against the hard cement as he walked toward the exit.

"Frankie, come back here!" his mother yelled, earning stern looks from the guards.

No, Frankie thought, shaking his head. *I'm never coming back here again!*

16

Friday afternoon, the Creech twins' beat-up Buick waited for Frankie in the Rondo parking lot. Coming out of the school at the end of the day were plenty of hard faces of all colors. Going into the ice rink part of the building were bright white faces with hockey gear. The contrast of colors, fates, and futures angered Frankie.

"Frankie!" Jay shouted from the driver's side.

Frankie looked over his shoulder. Where was Sofia? What if she saw him with the Creech twins and their sunglasses and gang tattoos?

"What are you doing here?" Frankie walked

over and leaned in the busted car window.

"You need more cigarettes to sell?" Billy asked. "You must be out, since no money is coming in."

"I'm shut down," Frankie told his cousins a false story about Mrs. Baker threatening to expel him for selling cigarettes on campus. It was really Sofia's words that had shut him down.

"So, big deal, they kick you out of school," Billy said. "We're dropping out soon."

Frankie knew better than to confess that he wasn't dropping out or that he liked Rondo. "I gotta go," he said.

"Come with us, we're headed to get more product," Jay said.

Frankie shook his head.

"Frankie, you scared? Don't worry. It's not another smash and grab," Billy said.

"Just busy," Frankie said. *Busy trying to change.*

"Really? My dad says you ain't been busy with what your old man told you to do," Jay said.

"Get in, Frankie," Billy said. "We're headed to Riverwood; you can see the fam."

Frankie thought of his grandfather's wise grin, so different from his father's battle-wrecked smile. He glanced around again and then got in the back seat.

17

Gus Tall Horse braided together the strands of sweetgrass effortlessly, like a man much younger. As Frankie sat by his grandfather's side in the small house, he tried to hide his smile. While his grandfather worked, Frankie knew his cousins were focused on another sacred plant: tobacco. There was no cigarette tax on the reservation, so the twins were buying up cigarettes at low cost to sell in St. Paul on the black market.

In a small alabaster bowl, a bundle of sage leaves burned, filling the air with the smell of fall. A musty cedar chest, open in the corner of the room, added to the aroma of the tiny space.

"You look tired, Frankie." His grandfather placed his hands on Frankie's sore shoulders.

Frankie laughed and then pointed outside at a large pile of rocks that he and his grandfather had spent the afternoon collecting. Rocks for the I-ni-pi, the sweat lodge ceremony, were symbols of the past.

"It's hard, being in a new city and school," Frankie said. His grandfather nodded like he understood. Frankie knew better: Gus had never left Riverwood in his life.

"You are a brave eagle. Spring is your time, not the fall. In spring, the whole world is starting over." They both sat silently for a moment before his grandfather continued. "Your mother writes me often. She says you're doing better in school, that's good."

Frankie nodded. "I guess so. It doesn't matter, though. Look at you."

His grandfather inhaled the smoky, sweet scents of the room deeply into his lungs. "Times have changed. Education matters more than it ever did. I'm proud of you, Frankie."

Don't be, Frankie thought to himself. In truth, he'd been spending more time with the Creech twins than with his schoolwork. He faked a smile to his grandfather, ashamed, and vowed to change.

18

Frankie's mom wasn't happy when he called to say he was staying in Riverwood for the weekend. In particular, she didn't like his ride. Frankie wished he could've driven to Riverwood on his own. But his mom's Ford was older and even more beat-up than the twins' ride. He didn't trust it to make it there.

"I stayed with Grandfather," Frankie said when he called his mom again Sunday, then quickly told his mom how he'd ditched his cousins after they got to the reservation. They'd agreed to take him on the return trip, provided that he find another place to sell their smokes. Frankie needed the ride.

"Still, you went without even talking to me first, and—" his mom started.

"I got no minutes left," Frankie said over her. "I'll see you at home."

"No, stop by the office."

"Your office? Why?"

There was silence, a sigh, and then she hissed, "Because I said so."

Frankie hung up.

Jay drove just below the speed limit down the highway. With the trunk and backseat stuffed with cigarettes, Frankie guessed they were breaking some law. It's what his cousins did. It's what his family did. "Frankie, what's your plan?" Jay asked.

"I don't know, maybe set up in my building or outside of school or—"

"Not about that, cuz, what are you doing about your dad?" Jay told Frankie what their father, also a First Nation Mafia chief imprisoned in Stillwater, had said about the fight and Frankie's duty to make it right. "Law of the jungle and law of the streets, right?"

Frankie wished the loud music was louder. He didn't want to hear this. If he didn't hear it, he didn't have to think about it.

"I don't believe in the eye for an eye," Jay said. "You gotta teach 'em respect. Take an eye? I say take a life." Jay glanced back at Frankie, reached into his coat pocket, and showed his cousin the Glock 9 handgun.

19

"Who are all these people?" Frankie whispered to his mother after making his way across the crowded office lobby. She ignored him and pointed toward the front of the room, where her boss commanded the group's attention.

Mrs. McCaskill, a short woman, said a prayer in Ojibwemowin and then repeated the prayer in English to the crowd of Ojibwe and Dakota women and children. "I pray our ancestors will help us solve our problems today."

Like the other children and teens, regardless of age, Frankie held his mom's hand. It was part of the smudging ceremony. Frankie listened as Mrs. McCaskill spoke, her voice cracking with emotion, about the community "left behind." Frankie's mom had helped organize the meeting of women who had relatives—children, husbands, fathers—inside prison walls.

"We must be purified of negative energy before we're ready to heal," Mrs. McCaskill said. "Only then we can gather with warm hearts and create a sacred space, to offer support to one another."

"Frankie, you do it." His mom gently pushed him toward the front of the room. Mrs. McCaskill handed Frankie a wooden match. Frankie lit the match and held it against a sage bundle resting in an abalone shell. As the sage burned, Frankie used a single black-and-white prayer feather with buckskin fringe and a handle wrapped with black sinew to fan the smoke toward his mother. She waved her hands in front of herself so that the smoke from the sage encompassed her body. His mother passed the shell and the feather to the next person. By the time it reached the last woman, a sweet, smoky sage fog enveloped the room. The faces of the twenty or so women turned peaceful.

As the sage burned, it reminded Frankie of all the weed he'd smoked in Riverwood, and he knew he wasn't ready to heal, much less help anyone else. His heart wasn't warm; it was stone cold.

20

Frankie stared into the mirror of the parked car outside Rondo. Tiny black shoots of hair poked from his scalp. His grandfather had shaved his head a lot better than his cousins had, but Frankie questioned his appearance. He wondered if it was really his looks, not his business, that Sofia found ugly. It was easy to go from there to questioning his whole identity. They'd watched *Hombre* last week, and Frankie felt like Paul Newman's character—stuck between the white world around him and the American Indian world within him.

"Go get 'em," he whispered to himself. A kid named Phil had planned a monster party for later that week. Frankie figured it was as good a shot as he'd have with Sofia.

He caught Luis in the parking lot just before classes started. "Did you tell Sofia that I'm not selling smokes anymore?" Frankie asked, almost pleading. "What did she say?"

"She says it's not what you do," Luis said. "It's who you are. That's how she sees you."

"But it is not—"

"Look, she jumped out. I don't know how Indians do it, but the Twenty-sixers . . . it ain't pretty."

Frankie shook his head in disgust at everyone and everything. He couldn't make anybody happy: the twins wanted him in deeper, while Sofia, his mom, and his grandfather didn't believe he wasn't in at all. "Tell her to give me one more chance. I like her, and she's worth it."

Luis started to laugh. "What's so funny?" Frankie snapped in anger.

More laughter, and then Luis said, "Why don't you turn around and tell her yourself?"

Frankie pivoted. Sofia stood behind him with a slight smile and a skeptical gaze.

"You got something to say to me?" Hands on hips, full of attitude and challenge.

"I'm like the hombre," Frankie said. "I used to be wild, but now I'm tame. Trust me."

21

"Frankie, a moment," Mrs. Howard-Hernandez said as Frankie started to leave the classroom, carefully watching Sofia exit.

After making him wait two days for an answer, Sofia had told him before class, "I won't go to the party with you, you know, but you can ride with me, Luis, and Jose." Frankie had daydreamed through class about the party's possibilities, but the teacher's words burst his bubble. She motioned for Frankie to sit in the chair next to her book-covered desk.

"About the book you chose for your next

project," Mrs. Howard-Hernandez said. "You can't do it."

"Why not?" Frankie expected a "because I said so," mom-like robot response.

"You've already read *The Outsiders*, many times, you said," his teacher explained. "For this assignment, I want you to read something new. Something you're interested in." Frankie nodded his head every few seconds as the teacher rattled off title after title, describing books that didn't interest him at all. He had to make her stop.

"Was that movie *Hombre* a book first?" he asked.

Mrs. Howard-Hernandez smiled briefly at him. "Let's see." She typed something on her keyboard as Frankie's mind wandered again. He had plenty more questions, none of which his teacher, her computer, or her beloved books could answer. How would he get out of being grounded to go to the party? His three-day Riverwood retreat had cost him two full weeks of not leaving home except for school. Well, not leaving home when his mom was awake. When she was asleep, Frankie went about his business, selling smokes by the west-side entrance to his building.

"Good news, Frankie. *Hombre* was based on a book, and they have it at the library!"

Frankie tried to manage a smile as he realized his next obstacle. After the stunt he'd pulled with the scissors, he thought, even getting his mom to let him go to the library might be tough.

22

"No."

"Why?"

"Because I said so."

"That's not a reason." The conversation between Frankie and his mom kept going in circles, always ending up at the same place: he couldn't go.

"If I go to the party, I'll make more new friends so I'm not hanging with Jay and Billy." Frankie couldn't confess that he already had a good reason to avoid the twins: the loaded Glock they carried.

"Well, I would be happy about that, but I know all about parties, Frankie. I was sixteen once you know."

"It won't be like that," Frankie pleaded, even though he figured it would be exactly like that.

"You know the destruction that chemical dependency has played in our community," his mom said, choking back tears. "The stories I hear every day would break your heart."

"I'm not like that anymore." Frankie looked his mom straight in the eye; for once, it wasn't a lie. He had also seen the devastating impact of drinking, using, and selling in his family, his reservation, and his tribe. "You can stay up late and give me one of those home drug tests afterward, but I really need this. *I need it.*"

Frankie's mom fiddled with her ID badge. "Okay, Frankie, but on one condition."

"Anything," Frankie said.

"You have to start visiting your father again," Frankie's mom said, meeting his eye. "He misses you."

Visions of his dad's eye patch stabbed Frankie's brain, but it was worth it to go to the party.

"I shouldn't have to bargain with you about seeing him," she said. "You should want to see him. I moved us here so you could visit him. Your uncles too. So, it's a deal?"

Frankie nodded. He tried to hide his nervousness that the deal was one he and his mom would both regret.

23

Like the week before, the Creech twins waited for Frankie in their car in the parking lot after school. Unlike the last time, Sofia, Luis, and Jose were with Frankie and got a good look at his relatives.

"Those look like some bad mo—" Jose started to say.

"Stay here. I'll talk to them." Frankie broke off from the group.

"You want me to get your back?" Luis said, hesitant.

"Don't need it. I got nothing to do with those

guys anymore." Frankie looked at Sofia the entire time he spoke. She appeared only half convinced.

Frankie walked slowly, head down, fists clenched. His friends spoke briefly in Spanish as they headed toward Jose's Impala.

By the time Frankie got to the Buick, Jay stood in front of it, pants hung low, head held high. "So, those your friends now?" Jay broke his hard stare only to glance at the Impala.

"What of it." Frankie glared back.

Billy came around behind Frankie. He was trapped. "Any of them Twenty-sixers?"

"No." Frankie lied. Luis worked and went to school full time. Jose's life was consumed with a disabled father, a job, and dealing with family problems. He was talking about dropping out. Sofia had been in the 26ers but said she'd left. Frankie didn't want to think about how.

"You gonna hang with friends over family, over tribe, over your people—"

"Shut up, Jay!" Frankie shouted.

"You're gonna have to make me, Frankie," Jay said as the twins closed like prison gates around Frankie.

From the corner of his eye, Frankie saw Jose's car speeding closer, back door open. Frankie pushed past his cousins and jumped into the Impala, his heart pounding.

24

"Did you know Phil had this kind of money?" Jose asked. Phil had thrown a monster party, as promised, that almost everyone in the school had shown up for. "He doesn't seem like a rich kid."

"And what kind of rich kid goes to Rondo?" Luis asked.

"Even if I had money, I'd still go to Rondo," Frankie said. "At Riverwood, everybody was the same, everybody was poor. If I went to a private high school with the rich white kids, everybody would be the same there too. Rondo's got a little bit of everything."

Sofia sipped a can of Diet Coke, so Frankie did the same. Luis slammed back strongly spiked punch from a red cup, while Jose stayed sober. Frankie listened as each person told their story. Just like Frankie, they'd failed in the past, and Rondo was a shot at starting over.

"You know, before they changed the name to Rondo, it just used to be called the ALC," Jose explained. A senior, he'd started at the alternative school in ninth grade. "The initials stood for alternative learning center, but everybody said it really meant assholes' last chance."

Luis laughed so hard he spilled his drink. "Come on, Jose, help me clean this up. It's your fault," Luis said, dragging Jose along and finally leaving Frankie alone with Sofia.

Frankie and Sofia took turns gulping their sodas rather than speaking.

"Thanks for letting me come with you," Frankie finally said. Sofia just smiled.

"I didn't want to say anything in front of them, but you're one of the biggest reasons I like Rondo," Frankie said.

“You say that ’cause you don’t know me. If—”

Sofia left off as they heard a wail of sirens coming closer. As people started panicking, Frankie reached out his hand, Sofia grabbed it, and they ran for the back door.

25

Frankie finally got to touch Sofia, but not as he'd imagined. He pushed her hard from behind to help her clear the high fence at the back of Phil's house.

"Run!" Sofia shouted. Frankie scaled the fence on his own and joined Sofia on the other side, in another huge backyard with a pool. "Let's go!"

Sofia took off her shoes and set off. Although no track star, Sofia could move. After two more yards, two more fences, and two more pushes, they came to an alley.

"I gotta stop." Frankie sat down on the cool pavement, panting. Sofia nodded and sat next to him.

"You've done this before, run from the cops?" she asked.

Frankie nodded.

"Me too, but no more."

"How about Jose or Luis?" Frankie asked. Sofia shook her head emphatically.

"Those boys got too much to do," Sofia said. "Luis with his job, or Jose and his father—if you got something that matters in your life, banging don't make sense."

"Maybe," Frankie said. He hesitated, but the time seemed right. He told her about his time in First Nation Mafia, his dad and his family's involvement, everything.

"That ain't nothing," Sofia countered and told her war stories of being in the 26ers. "But I left all that. I came to Rondo for a new school, making new friends, like I'm starting over."

"Starting over," Frankie echoed. "Me too."

"Like with your hair?" Sophie laughed. Frankie laughed too as he placed her left hand on his bald head. "I should check in with Luis. See if they got away."

"Or we could stay here until they call." Sofia said with a small smile. Her left hand fell from Frankie's head to his neck and pulled him in for a kiss.

26

“Look at me!” Frankie’s father shouted so loud that he didn’t need the inmate phone.

Frankie tried, but he couldn’t bring himself to focus on his father’s face with the pinkish eye patch still covering the hole where his eye had been.

“What is wrong with you?” The guards strolled slowly toward Franklin Brave Eagle like children afraid of a dog. They spoke with him, but his father just shouted.

“Let me talk to him,” Frankie’s mother said. Frankie handed her the phone and stepped away. He didn't want to listen to his mother, much less his father. His father had told Frankie that he had to act. If word got back that there was no retaliation, then all members of the First Nation Mafia in Stillwater were targets. Inside or outside didn't matter—all that mattered was respect and revenge.

Frankie placed his right hand over his mouth, brushing against his lips. Just last night, Sofia had kissed those lips, and everything seemed softer. But looking at his father's disfigured face, Frankie realized last night was just an illusion. This nightmare was his life; this reality was his legacy.

"He wants to talk to you." Frankie's mom handed him back the phone. It was wet with tears.

"Listen, son," Frankie's father started, but then stopped. "You like that word, *son*? Well, you're not my son anymore," his father hissed. "Jay and Billy, those boys know their responsibilities to their family and their tribe. But you don't seem to, Frankie."

Frankie tried to argue, tried to prove his

father was wrong. But even though the phone was at his ear, his dad wasn't listening. He had made it clear what Frankie had to do to prove himself.

27

"I don't want to visit him again tomorrow." Frankie slammed the car door after getting in, anxious to drive away from the Stillwater prison.

"You promised," his mom said.

"I need to talk to Grandfather." Frankie started to dial his prepaid cell number.

"You know my father would rather dance naked than talk on the phone." His mom laughed as she turned the key to start the engine. But the laughter ended as the engine turned over briefly and sputtered out. Frankie heard her curse under her breath.

"Then let's go see him," Frankie pleaded. He knew he sounded like a spoiled child, but he felt like a child asked to take on too much too soon.

"This car may not make it back to St. Paul, let alone all the way to Riverwood."

"We could rent a car," Frankie said softly. He clutched the wad of bills in his pocket.

Another laugh. "With what?"

Frankie showed his mom the money as he told her the story about smuggling cigarettes from Riverwood to sell in St. Paul. He didn't mention the smash and grab from earlier. Still, his mother fumed.

"Look, I'm done with it," Frankie said.

"You've said that before, and then you tell me this. Why should I believe you?"

"Sofia, she's this girl—" and the words poured out as Frankie talked about Sofia like he'd never talked about a girl before. His mom was stunned.

"Don't talk so fast, Frankie," his mom said, trying to catch up, trying the ignition again. The engine roared but didn't purr.

Frankie rolled his eyes and laughed. "Normally you're mad because I don't talk to you. Now I do, and you tell me to slow down."

"We've got time," his mom said. She drew in a big breath. "It's a long drive to Riverwood, even in a rented car."

28

"Next time, Frankie, you need to stay longer." Frankie and his grandfather stood on a small hill at the end of a dirt road. Each of them carried a large sack of rocks and stones.

"Um. Yeah. I hope so." Frankie wasn't sure how to answer. Life in Riverwood moved so slowly, and most everything his grandfather did connected to ancient traditions. His grandfather rejected almost anything modern. He wouldn't allow Frankie to listen to music or talk on the phone in his house.

"I know that tone, Frankie." His grandfather

pulled Frankie next to him.

"Sorry," Frankie mumbled. "I just got a lot on my mind."

"Exactly. When you come again, we will clear your mind and purify your body."

Frankie snorted. "Not another vision quest?"

His grandfather laughed, not the most common of sounds. "No, that didn't work out."

When he first started to get into trouble, Frankie's grandfather had intervened and forced Frankie—by the power of his personality—to embark on a vision quest. Frankie was sent off for four days and nights to sit by himself on the top of the hill. With no food or water, and just a ceremonial buckskin skirt, Frankie was told to wait for the insight that his grandfather said would emerge.

But after four days, when his grandfather came to retrieve him, he found that Frankie had violated the most sacred part of the ritual: he had not been alone. Someone—Frankie never told who—had brought food and water, and more. His grandfather saw the truth in Frankie's bloodshot eyes. For the first time ever, his grandfather had struck him hard across the face with the back of his hand. Frankie remembered how the blood had dripped down his nose onto his left arm, newly decorated with a First Nation Mafia tattoo.

"I wasn't ready," Frankie explained. "A ceremony must come from within, right?"

His grandfather nodded. "When you are ready, your eyes will see."

29

"Mrs. Smith, nice to see you again," Mrs. Howard-Hernandez said as Frankie's mom took a seat in the chair on the other side of the desk. Frankie took the chair next to her.

"You remember Mr. Aaron, our educational assistant," Frankie's teacher said. Mr. Aaron nodded and sat down next to her, and his dreads shook. "Principal Baker might be stopping by if she has time. This is always a busy night at Rondo."

Frankie looked oddly at his teacher. Busy? He'd seen few parents and students when they arrived. Sofia was with her mother, and Luis was with his dad. Jose had dropped out of school to work.

"Frankie has turned out to be delight," Mrs. Howard-Hernandez said. "I thought we'd have more of a challenge with Frankie when he announced his hatred of reading, but—"

"I didn't say I hated it," Frankie blurted. "I didn't like it 'cause I'm not good at it, and every class they just give me something dumb to read."

"He did a nice oral report based on the book *The Outsiders*," his teacher said. "For the semester project, he'll answer exam questions on a book called *Hombre*, by Elmore Leonard."

Frankie didn't mention he'd yet to get the book from the library, since he'd learned the library was in the 26ers' domain. He figured he might as well wear a target on his back in 26er territory.

"What are your plans after high school, Frankie?" Mr. Aaron asked. "College? A family business?"

"College," Frankie said, to his mom's obvious surprise.

"I'm glad to hear you say that," Mr. Aaron said. "Got any idea which one?"

Frankie didn't know anything about college except one thing: Sofia was going.

"I would love to see him go to college," his mom said. "I don't know how we'll afford it, but I'll help you get wherever you want to be, Frankie." She paused as her eyes welled up and her voice caught. "Anywhere other than Stillwater."

30

Sofia and Frankie sat across from each other in a diner located in a run-down strip mall halfway between St. Paul and Stillwater. Maybe because it was failing, neither First Nation Mafia nor the 26ers claimed it as their turf. “Did you hear about Armando?” Sofia asked.

“What happened?” Frankie sipped his milkshake with his right hand and inched closer to Sofia. Under the table, his left hand and hers intertwined.

“He got shot outside the library.” Sofia told Frankie how Armando, a friend of hers who had graduated from Rondo last year, was killed in a drive-by the previous night.

"Do they know who did it?" Frankie dreaded the answer. *Don't say two guys in sunglasses driving a beat-up Buick*, he thought. "Or why? Was it one of the gangs?"

"The Twenty-sixers and First Nation Mafia have been going at it for years—it ain't never gonna end," Sofia said, a deep sadness in her voice. Frankie squeezed her hand tight.

"Eye for an eye," Frankie mumbled.

"I'm so glad to be away from all of that." She took a sip of her shake.

Frankie wanted to ask how she jumped out. But once again, he dreaded the answer.

"All that blood, and for what? Nothing changes. Just keep having more funerals." Sofia looked Frankie in the eye. "I'm glad you're not hanging with your cousins anymore," she said.

Frankie smiled, just a little. "I found somebody much better to be with."

"We're lucky to get out," Sofia said. "The thing about eye for an eye, it never ends."

Frankie thought how much he wished that

weren't true, for his own sake. "Never?"

Sofia gazed at Frankie with her big brown eyes. She shrugged. "I guess when everybody is blind."

31

Mrs. Howard-Hernandez gave Frankie a kind smile. "I understand about library fines, I've had some myself," she said.

Frankie felt bad lying to her, especially after she'd said all those nice things about him on parent-teacher night. But lying about the reason he needed her to pick up his library book shouldn't matter, he figured. No way did he want to end up like Armando. Since the Mafia had hit a 26er, the 26ers would be looking for revenge on the same turf.

"So, could you get the book for me?" Frankie asked.

"I'd better do it quickly. The term is almost up. I want to make sure you stay on track to graduate in the spring."

"Graduate," Frankie repeated. It had never seemed so close.

"You know, some of our students earn enough credits to graduate after the first semester—especially if it's their fifth year of high school. At the end of this term, we'll have a ceremony to celebrate. All students and families are invited. You should come, to see what it's like."

"I know what ceremonies are like. There's a lot of that in my culture," Frankie said. Those ceremonies and big events, and his grandfather, were a few of the things he missed about Riverwood.

"Will you tell me more about them?" Mrs. Howard-Hernandez asked. But Frankie didn't want to talk about it. He wanted to live it. He needed to get back to his grandfather at Riverwood. He was ready to open his eyes.

"Frankie?"

"Sorry, I was just, um, I was thinking about

what book I should read after *Hombre*. What do you think?"

His trick worked to distract Mrs. Howard-Hernandez. As she was off and running with ideas for Frankie, he concentrated on a plan for his next visit to the reservation. He was ready for the I-ni-pi, the purification ceremony.

32

"Time's up," Jay said as he and Billy barged into Frankie's apartment without an invite.

"If you don't do it, we will," Billy added as he pushed past Frankie toward the sofa.

I don't want this, Frankie thought, *I don't need this. Not now, not ever again.*

It was the day before finals, and Frankie had just finished reading *Hombre*. To make sure no one cheated on their book report, the final in language arts was to answer questions about their book, on specific elements as well as what his teacher called "big themes."

"What is this garbage?" Jay grabbed the book and held it high in the air. "*Hombre*? Serious?"

Billy laughed when Jay passed the book over to him. "Put it down," Frankie said.

"You don't have your Twenty-sixer friends to save you now," Billy countered.

"I told you, those people at school, they're not in the Twenty-sixers," Frankie said. "I thought this was over with. Didn't one of them get shot at the library? Doesn't that even things up?"

"That's about business." Jay bounced the book in his hand. "This is different. It's payback. It's personal. This kid's got it coming, the nephew of the guy who did your dad."

Frankie thought of his talk with Sofia the other night. He didn't want to be responsible for another "eye for an eye."

"No, I won't do it," Frankie said. He clenched his fists tighter, while his body braced for a blow.

"Fine, we can do it. But if it's up to us, we're not just messin' him up. He's not walking outta there alive," Jay said.

"Who is he?"

"He goes to your school. You might know him."

"Who?"

The twins laughed. "Luis Martinez."

Frankie tried to stay calm. "He's not a Twenty-sixer."

"His uncle is. Family ties are close enough."

As Jay placed a heavy Glock in Frankie's hand, the weight of family duty felt even heavier.

33

"Time's up!" Mrs. Howard-Hernandez shouted. Frankie set down his pen and looked at the pages of his blue book, filled with his thoughts not just about *Hombre* but about the "big theme" of identity. School gave him a final exam to test his mind; the sweat lodge in a few days would challenge his body and spirit, his own identity.

Sofia smiled at Frankie; she must have done well on the test too. Luis didn't look as happy.

Frankie knew that whether Luis ever smiled or breathed again might rest in his hands.

The rest of his finals were harder, mainly

because language arts had somehow become Frankie's favorite class, something he never would've imagined. But most of Rondo had turned out that way. He was prepared to hate it and had grown to like it. Prepared to fail, Frankie had succeeded. He knew he'd pass every class when grades came out. He had started over.

After school on the last day of finals, Frankie sat in the passenger seat of Sofia's car. "Sofia, stay with me." Frankie wouldn't take a ride home from her, for both their safety. "I'm waiting for my mom to pick me up in an hour, and then we're going straight to Riverwood for the break."

"Don't go, I'll miss you." Sofia ran her hands over his stubbly head. "Why do you have to be there so long?"

Frankie took her hand and explained the I-ni-pi ceremony as best he could.

"It sounds really hard. Why would you put yourself through that?" Sofia asked.

Frankie pulled her tight. "For the same reason you put yourself through what you had to do to get out of the Twenty-sixers. I don't care what, and I don't want to know, unless you want to tell me."

Sofia started to speak, but the tears came too fast, too hard.

"I'll think of you during the I-ni-pi," Frankie said. "And we'll both be purified again."

34

Without a word, Frankie's grandfather handed him the last heavy deer-hide blanket to place over the saplings to complete the sweat lodge they would soon enter. Many times, Frankie had helped his grandfather build the lodge for the I-ni-pi ceremony, but always for others. In the background, a single drum pounded rhythmically.

"Should I—" Frankie started, but his grandfather's harsh scowl shut him up. Frankie couldn't recall the last time he'd gone four hours without speaking. With no words leaving his mouth, thoughts piled up in his head, heavy as the stones he'd soon carry inside.

Stripped to just a pair of shorts, Frankie and the other young men gathered by the fire pit. Frankie knew these boys from the life he'd left behind. He was the only one without a First Nation Mafia tattoo showing on his bare arms. Frankie noticed that the opening of the ceremonial structure faced southeast, toward St. Paul and Stillwater.

After Frankie's grandfather finished another prayer, he gathered two stones with sharp edges. It only took him only one try to create the spark and start the blaze in the fire pit. As the kindling burned, the stones Frankie and the others had collected began to warm. The fire grew higher and hotter, but mostly louder as the snap, crackle, and pop of stones increased. All of the boys tossed gifts to the spirits—sage, sweet-grass, tobacco, and cedar—onto the fire. The smell of the fire woke up all of Frankie's senses.

Frankie was the last called into the lodge, but first to pour water over the steaming rocks they'd carried inside. The steam blinded

Frankie as it filled the lodge; as he adjusted to it, his cleansed-self vision became crystal clear.

35

Everyone in the St. Paul Central High School gym was smiling. Frankie's mom turned to the family of a graduating student and congratulated them in broken Spanish. People stood taking pictures, capturing the moment their children turned into adults, signified by a high school diploma in hand.

The gym was crowded with all the Rondo students and their families. Mrs. Howard-Hernandez hadn't lied: this was a big deal for everyone.

"Mom, I'd like you to meet someone," Frankie said.

"*Enhorabuena!*" his mom said again and then joined Frankie. Across the room stood Sofia with her mom. No dad. There was no need to ask.

The laughter of happy families washed over Frankie, and his newly purified skin soaked up the joy like a thirsty sponge. "Mom, this is my friend Sofia," Frankie said. Sofia blushed almost as much as he did.

Frankie's mom and Sofia's mom burst out together in laughter. "Nice to see you again." Frankie's mom extended her hand. Sofia's mom shook it, like they were old friends.

"What's so funny?" Frankie asked. *And what did "see you again" mean?* he added silently.

"I think the two of you are a little more than friends," Sofia's mother said.

Sofia stepped closer to Frankie, hands outstretched. Frankie let them drop into his palms. "There's a connection between girls and moms," Sofia said.

Frankie said nothing, but guided Sofia away from their mothers.

The two women talked and laughed. Frankie was riveted to Sofia's every word but was distracted when he heard Sofia's mom say, "And this is my nephew, Luis Martinez. Next year, he'll get a diploma. He's got his whole life in front of him."

36

"Where does this Martinez kid live?" Jay asked Frankie.

Frankie gave him the address. Billy turned around. "It's your lucky day, cuz," he said, and he handed Frankie a gun. His father's gun, the pearl-handled revolver from his dresser. "Even sweeter revenge than with the Glock."

Frankie eyed Billy suspiciously.

"You shouldn't leave such pretty things lying around your room," Billy replied.

"About time, Frankie," Jay said. "If you weren't family, cuz, no way would we have waited this long."

"I was trying to start over," Frankie mumbled. The Buick sped through the crowded St. Paul streets until Frankie yelled, "Jay, where you going? This isn't the right direction!"

Jay cursed over Frankie telling him the route Frankie wanted him to take. About a block away, near a stretch of vacant houses, Frankie asked Jay to pull the car over. The houses were alive with layer after layer of spray paint, each gang claiming the area, then another taking it back.

Frankie stayed calm even as he looked at the top layer: this was 26ers turf.

"What are we doing here?" Jay asked.

"Stop the car and get out!" Frankie shouted.

"You crazy, cuz, this is Twenty-sixers', I'm not getting out in this—"

The Glock in Frankie's left hand set against the back of Jay's head shut him up, fast.

"What are you doing?" Billy turned around. The barrel of the pearl-handled revolver in Frankie's right hand pointed at Billy's face had the same silencing effect. Jay stopped the car.

"Get out!" Frankie repeated. "Jay, you first,

then you, Billy. Don't make me do this."

"Cuz, you ain't gonna—" the cocking sound of the revolver ended Billy's argument.

"Leave the car running," Frankie commanded. Jay did as he was told.

Billy spat on the ground. "Frankie, I don't know what you think you're doing, but—"

Frankie cut him off. "I know what I'm doing and who I am. A brave eagle. This ends tonight." With a steady hand pointed at Jay, Frankie pulled the trigger of the Glock.

37

Because Frankie had called ahead, Luis and Sofia were ready by the curb of her home when Frankie pulled up well after midnight. Luis started to make jokes as he climbed into the backseat of the Buick, but Frankie shut him down.

"Shut up, Luis!" Frankie yelled, his throat dry from stress and smoke.

"Where are we going?" Sofia asked. She'd asked on the phone too, but Frankie wouldn't answer. Sofia curled up next to Frankie, who drove slow but steady. It had been a while since he'd driven, but some things a person doesn't forget, like how to drive a car or how to fire a pistol.

"I don't understand, what this is about?" Luis asked.

"Just wait," Frankie said as they made their way out of St. Paul and through Minneapolis to head west toward Riverwood.

"This is what it's about." Frankie reached under his seat and pulled out the revolver.

"What are you doing with a gun?" Sofia asked. "You said that you weren't—"

Frankie cut her off quickly. "It's not mine. This is my father's gun."

"What are you doing with it?" Luis asked. Frankie didn't answer right away. He pulled Sofia into his right side, while his left side was weighted down by the six bullets he'd taken from the Glock. He'd taken his cousins' car and bullets, but left them with an empty gun in 26ers territory. Frankie hoped the twins were ready to gain something from their urban vision quest.

"Frankie, answer Luis," Sofia whispered, concerned. Frankie took a deep breath and told them both about his father's injured eye and quest for revenge against Luis's uncle. Frankie told Luis about his father's role in the First Nation Mafia and his history of crime in Riverwood and in St. Paul. As Frankie spoke, it reminded him of writing his final exam. A person only understood themselves when they looked inside. Frankie hoped that, even half blind, his father could find the insight to turn his life around and not drown in the dark revenge culture of Stillwater State Prison.

38

After a nap at a rest stop, Frankie pulled into the Riverwood Reservation and his grandfather's driveway just before sunrise. He left Sofia and Luis sleeping in the car as he went in to wake his grandfather.

"Grandfather I need you!" Frankie knocked on the door.

Minutes later, the door opened slowly, and his grandfather moved slower. "Frankie, I was not expecting you. Come inside. Does your mother know you are here?"

"Yes." He hoped it was the last time he'd

have to lie to his grandfather.

"What brings you here?"

"I need your help. I need you to say this prayer." Frankie handed him the framed Yellow Lark prayer.

Gus looked at Frankie and out toward the car, concerned. "Is everyone OK?"

"We're all fine," Frankie said. "But I need to do something. Kind of . . . a funeral."

The old man got dressed while Frankie went outside, dug a small hole in the ground, and summoned Luis and Sofia from the car. A cold early morning wind chilled Frankie as the four of them stood by the small, empty grave. As his grandfather began to speak, Frankie bowed his head, letting the tears touch the ground quicker.

"Oh, Great Spirit, whose voice I hear in the winds and whose breath gives life to all the world, hear me. I am small and weak. I need your strength and wisdom. Let me walk in beauty, and make my eyes ever behold the red and purple sunset. Make my hands respectful of the things you have made and my ears sharp to hear your voice. Make me wise so that I may understand the things you have taught my people. Let me learn the lessons you have hidden in every leaf and rock. I seek strength, not to be stronger than my brother, but to fight my greatest enemy—myself. Make me ready to come to you with clean hands and straight eyes, so when life fades, as the fading sunset, my spirit will come to you without shame."

After the final words, Freddie dropped the pearl-handled revolver—and everything it represented in his family's life—into the ground and gently kicked the dirt over his father's gun.

39

After seeking his grandfather's wisdom, Frankie had called his mom, seeking forgiveness. To do so, she said, he first needed to confess his wrongs. As he did, his mom's reactions wavered from sighs to the occasional, "Why, Frankie, why?" He'd had his mom check on the twins, who had made it home alive, which meant Frankie and his mom might not be safe. The only choice, it seemed, was to move again. As Frankie drove back from Riverwood, his mom found them a place much closer to her work and Rondo, but much farther from the prison.

Back in St. Paul that evening, Frankie dropped Sofia off first. Once she had left the car, Luis spoke up. "Thanks, bro."

Frankie's fist bumped his. "It's got to end with us," Frankie said. "Or we'll be just like the rest of our family, going through the prison's revolving doors."

When Frankie got back to his building, his mom was waiting out front for him.

"Frankie, I'm so glad you're home." His mom ran her hands over her son's head of hair, slowly growing back in, as she climbed into the car. He looked like himself again.

"Can we find a library by the new apartment?" Frankie asked. She nodded.

"Can I ask something else?" Another nod. "Why are we moving farther away from Dad?"

She hesitated.

"I mean, I thought we moved here because you wanted me to see him."

Frankie saw her fighting back tears. Finally she answered.

"A true brave eagle wouldn't live in a cage. You needed to see his cage," his mom said.

"You just wanted me to see the prison?" Frankie mumbled, confused.

She was clear-eyed now. "The path you were on, the friends you had, the choices you made," she said. "We didn't move here so you could see your father. We moved here so you could see your future, Frankie. And change it."

AUTHOR'S NOTE

As I was researching this book, I found several articles in the Minneapolis and St. Paul newspapers about imprisonment of leaders of the Native Mob gang. In the past, whenever there was a crackdown on gang leaders, it cooled gang activity for a while as younger gang members fought for control.

Around the same time, I observed a large influx of American Indian men and boys in the short-term county correctional facilities where I work. These were men I'd seen before: for them, the prison gates they kept entering year after year, generation and generation, were like a revolving door. While there are many factors that cause this phenomenon, perhaps two key ones are generational poverty coupled with the disgraceful history of the treatment of the United States' native peoples.

The prayer in chapter 38 is from Chief Yellow Lark, ca. 1887. It can be found in *Honoring the Medicine: The Essential Guide to Native American Healing*, by Kenneth Cohen (New York: Ballantine Books, 2003, p. 193).

It is always tricky to write about or from the point of view of a different culture. In this book, I tried to be sensitive in portraying American Indian culture. In addition to my own research, Brent Chartier, who has coauthored books with me, brought his expertise around ceremonies such as smudging from his time working at an American Indian health clinic in Michigan.

Finally, as with all the books in The Alternative series, thanks go to the students and teachers at South Saint Paul Community Learning Center who read and commented on the manuscript, in particular John Egelkrout, Mindy Haukedahl, Kathleen Johnson, and Lisa Seppelt.

ABOUT THE AUTHOR

Patrick Jones is the author of more than twenty novels for teens. He has also written two nonfiction books about combat sports: *The Main Event*, on professional wrestling, and *Ultimate Fighting*, on mixed martial arts. He has spoken to students at more than one hundred alternative schools, including residents of juvenile correctional facilities. Find him on the web at www.connectingya.com and on Twitter: @PatrickJonesYA.

THE ALTERNATIVE

FAILING CLASSES.

DROPPING OUT.

JAIL TIME.

When it seems like there are no other options left, Rondo Alternative High School might just be the last chance a student needs.

WELCOME TO

LEARN TO FIGHT,
LEARN TO LIVE,
AND LEARN
TO FIGHT
FOR YOUR
LIFE.